Chilled

Anne Eton

This paperback is also available as an ebook at most online ebook retailers.

Copyright 2013 Beginnings Press

ISBN-13: 978-1-62602-026-9

ISBN-10: 1626020264

"Once again, a cold front coming down northern Massachusetts should hit the Wellesley area in just a few hours. So if you are inside, you might want to stay inside…"

None of the girls paid attention to the local television news. Everyone in the dorm room was too busy enjoying the party. All of the attendees (and there were, as usual, only female attendees) were focused upon a circle of young women sitting cross-legged on the floor. The standing observers were squealing, shouting encouragement, and drinking. Most had been drinking since noon.

Tracy, one of the two co-hosts, had minutes earlier shouted to the group: "Okay you guys, time for the Linda Lovelace Challenge." Tracy explained to those who did not get the reference that Linda Lovelace was a '70s porn star, best known for her movie *Deep Throat*. It was said that

Linda could swallow even the most well-endowed man; and all the way down, at that.

Tracy withdrew an uncommonly long zucchini from her refrigerator. After warming it to room temperature on the "defrost" setting in a microwave, she had carefully marked off inches on the vegetable with a sharpie and a kitchen ruler, to the cheers of the assembled ladies. A few who accepted Tracy's challenge sat on the floor in a circle per her instructions. The others stood, watching.

"Uh. Can we, kind of, like, wash it or something?" asked the first participant, a brunette wearing a Wellesley College Widows t-shirt.

"Why certainly, young lady," jeered an inebriated friend, standing and watching from above. The friend affected a man's deep voice: "'I will be more than happy to go into the bathroom and wash my dick off before you place it into your oh-so-sanitary amuse-bouche!'"

The girls howled. Amid the din the contestant looked at the floor, smiling sheepishly. She raised the zucchini. "You are absolutely right," she said. "I have swallowed way, way more… unsanitary things than this!" Without further ado, she closed her eyes and began sliding the vegetable into her mouth. The crowd chanted numbers as the inch-marks disappeared past her lips: "One!… Two!… Three!…"

The girl only made it to five inches. Amid general laughter and cries of "Weak!", she handed off the zucchini to the next girl, a chubby redhead with glasses. The redhead brushed her hair from her face with great authority, wiped the vegetable on her shirt, and opened her mouth.

Small, pale Dominika Staniszewski hung back as usual, sitting in a chair near the back, alternately cursing her shyness and wondering at the Linda Lovelace Challenge. She touched her long blonde locks, mimicking the redhead's confident hair-toss. In her small town in Poland, girls and women never discussed such things as fellatio. Growing up, Dominika had not even known such things existed. And that partly was why she had come to America.

* * *

Growing up in Tarnów, Dominika had achieved minor celebrity as The Driven Girl. She had worked harder than anyone at her school, had fearlessly written to every grant and scholarship fund she could find, and had finally achieved her dream: full scholarship at an American college, Wellesley as it turned out, an all-girls' school.

Her parents would not agree to her leaving Poland unless the college Dominika attended was women only; Mr. and Mrs. Staniszewski were very Old World in their attitudes and anxieties for their only child. And so the dutiful daughter had applied only to single-sex colleges and universities. At the time, Dominika had not thought it a major inconvenience. She had always been too busy to think about boys. There would be plenty of time for a husband later, perhaps after she had earned a medical degree.

And yet Dominika had not been prepared for the hypersexualized culture of American society. It seemed that at Wellesley, boys and sex were all that her fellow students talked about. On her first day as a freshman, the very first thing the shocked Polish girl had been briefed on by her new roommate was the schedule of the "Fuck Truck," a shuttle bus that ran a continuous circuit from Wellesley to Harvard to MIT and back to Wellesley.

"This shuttle," Dominika had stuttered. "It is called... what?"

"The Fuck Truck," her freshman roommate, a skinny gum-chewing girl named Maggie, had repeated. "Like, if you wanna fuck, you get on the truck."

Dominika had stared.

"Of course that's not its REAL name," Maggie had continued. "It's really called like, the shuttle whatever. It's allegedly for girls who want to go study at the Harvard and MIT libraries. But it's really there for the fuck thing. You know? If we didn't have some kind of way to get us out to some men once and a while, every bitch here would burn this campus down." Maggie had then begun explaining how the easiest and cheapest way to get laid was to get invited to a party by boys at a co-ed college, and you could get invited to a party by dressing hot and hanging out at that campus' coffee shops, sundry stores, campus lounges…

Dominika discovered she had a lot to learn about America.

And yet, once she had recovered from her shock, Dominika considered that all this was a good thing. Had she not worked so hard to get out of Poland for precisely the reason that her hometown was so provincial, conservative and unworldly? Dominika had wanted to experience life. Real life. And she knew that the only way was to push herself forward, overcome her natural inclination to hang back.

And so once she arrived, she joined the Wellesley College Widows, the campus a cappella singing group. She could not sing, or at least, she didn't know if she could; it was something she had never attempted in Poland. The thought of harmonizing with girls who were much better than her, in English, in front of an audience no less, made her feel faint. And it was precisely for this reason that she had auditioned. She had discovered to her surprise that she had a passable soprano voice, and if her Polish accent in conversation sometimes mystified her fellow choirists, the accent never manifested itself when she sang. She made friends. Plus, Dominika loved the sleeveless all-black outfits.

Years passed quickly. As she began her senior

year, Dominika believed that she had finally acclimated to American society. She had gotten used to sex being the number-one topic of conversation among her Wellesley friends, and had even grown comfortable enough with the subject that she joked and teased her friends back whenever they called her by her nickname, PDS ("Pure as the Driven Snow"). Dominika had never once boarded the Fuck Truck, even to visit another library. That's what interlibrary loan was for.

The Polish girl's singing improved to the point where she sang in the shower, just for the pleasure of hearing her own voice. She was so proud of herself for accomplishing her goal of pushing herself forward that she decided to do what previously would have been unthinkable.

She would act in a play.

The Polish girl had never acted before. The idea of saying lines, in her thick accent, on a stage with perhaps hundreds of people watching her every move, created a tightness in her throat and a throbbing in her head whenever she thought about it. And yet it was now or never. She had already been accepted to the best medical school in Poland, much to the great joy and relief of her parents. If she was ever truly going to push her boundaries and see what she was capable of, she needed to do it this year, her senior year.

And so Dominika found herself walking into the building that housed the theater department.

Once inside she followed signs pointing to auditions. A new production of Othello had been announced in the school paper, and all Wellesley students were invited to try out. The blonde had thought that perhaps she could get a small part, a walk-on role maybe.

Dominika entered a hall that was deserted except for a lone black girl reading behind a folding table. As the blonde approached, the black girl looked up, saw her, and shouted back over her shoulder: "We have our Desdemona."

In short order Dominika found herself sitting with the girls of the theater production. They all eyed her intently. Dominika wished she could disappear into the floor.

"So you have no acting experience?" asked a girl who had earlier identified herself as the director.

"Yes, that is correct," the Polish girl had replied in a whisper.

The director looked around. "Anybody have a problem with casting her as Desdemona?"

The girls all shook their heads. No problem.

"I am sorry," Dominika said, "but I do not understand. I believe this is a major role. I have never been on stage before, indeed I do not know if I may have stage fright. I was hoping only for a small part..."

"You're perfect," interrupted a short girl with thick frizzy hair.

"Yeah," said another. "You look more like

Desdemona than Desdemona. Archetypal blonde hair, blue eyes, white skin… And you look so shy. You look like an angel."

Dominika looked down and flushed up to her roots.

"I wish Gina was here," the director said. She added, as an aside to Dominika: "She's playing Othello."

"Gina will totally agree," someone said.

"Maybe. It's really her call," warned another voice.

"If I may," Dominika asked. She forced herself to look up. "There are other girls on this campus who look like me. With the blonde hair, and things like that. Why do you not cast them?"

"They're not auditioning," said the director.

A girl who had not spoken before nodded her head. "And besides…"

She paused, hesitating. Finally, she continued: "Okay, I'll say it. You just seem really, really innocent."

The other girls nodded solemnly.

Dominika turned red again, this time from anger. "I am not so innocent. I am not!"

"Are you a virgin?" the director asked.

Dominika's jaw dropped. She opened her mouth wider to make a reply, then closed it.

The director turned to the others. "Gina will be here for rehearsal tonight, right?" Off their nods, the director turned again to Dominika. "Seven o'clock, downstairs. Bring some food, we might go late."

That night, Dominika was on stage scanning what seemed to her to be an endless number of script pages when she heard voices all around shout: "Hail, Othello!"

Dominika turned around. A beautiful tall girl with long black curly hair and olive skin strode up the aisle toward them, smiling. She lifted a hand in greeting, but said nothing. Even though she wore only a t-shirt and jeans, the carriage of her walk and the way she held her head and shoulders communicated a strong, charismatic personality. Dominika could discern an hourglass shape under the baggy clothes.

The tall girl hopped up the steps with a loping athletic stride. The director hurried over to her.

"Hey Gina," the director said.

"Hey," the tall girl replied. "Is this her?"

The director said yes.

Gina turned her gaze to Dominika, sizing her up and down. She finally nodded. "Okay."

And that was that.

It took all of Dominika's scheduling skill to maintain her grades while simultaneously performing with the Widows and attending nightly rehearsals with the Shakespeare Society. But she did not complain. Indeed, she quickly thought herself lucky to be performing with an actor of Gina's caliber. Everyone in the theater company deferred to her, and Dominika understood immediately why the girl had been cast as Othello: in addition to her talent, Gina was sexy, confident and cool without being haughty. She never seemed to make a wrong creative decision wherever the play was concerned. Her charisma radiated from the stage; during her scenes, everyone would stop what they were doing just to watch her perform. It was like watching a young, female Marlon Brando.

The only thing that broke up the good-vibe camaraderie of the troupe was whenever Gina's girlfriend Annabelle visited. Annabelle was tall, blonde, and gorgeous, a Hitchcock blonde. The Dallas beauty queen's beauty ran cold. And her iciness only seemed to make Gina hot, under the collar anyway; Gina only ever lost her composure when she got into an argument with Annabelle. And that seemed to be on every occasion that Annabelle visited the theatre.

"Don't talk to me that way," Annabelle had shouted at Gina only a few days into rehearsals. The other girls had dropped their eyes and pretended that they were busy, trying to give Gina and her girlfriend a respectful privacy that was impossible.

"I'm not talking to you any way," Gina had replied, her voice rising.

"Yes you are! That tone."

"Can we just save the drama till later? I've got enough here."

"Well excuse me. I was just the one who was trying to tell you I cared. But obviously you don't care that I care." Annabelle had turned on her heel and walked out. Gina watched her leave.

After a long pause, the director had announced: "Okay, coffee break. Five minutes, then let's go from the top of Act Three again."

By this time, Dominika was used to the idea of a girl dating another girl. It was an inescapable fact of life at Wellesley. Gay, Lesbian, Bi, Transgender, Queer, Dyke, Butch, Femme—the formerly clueless young Polish lady was now familiar with all the academic terms, and what they meant. Still, a girl dating a girl seemed very foreign to her. If such things happened in Poland, the relationships were very much underground. Dominika wasn't even sure how it worked. There was something about Tribbing, she suspected; she had overheard LGBT girls talk about Tribbing. But she didn't know what it was, and was too embarrassed to ask. She didn't google it either. The girl had a feeling that it was some kind of very sexual thing, and very sexual things made her uncomfortable.

Dominika had grown to enjoy the play rehearsals, so much that she would hurry to the theatre building, leaning forward, walking as fast as she could without running. She had become mesmerized by Gina, like every other girl in the production.

Dominika found herself bending over backward to try to please Gina, studying the taller girl's every expression to try to discern even the subtlest hint of what made her happy and what did not. The blonde made it a point to learn her lines perfectly, but she feared her delivery was all wrong.

"Am I saying 'thou' correctly?" she once asked Gina during a break.

"Huh?"

"Am I saying 'thou' correctly," Dominika had repeated. "I think maybe I am saying 'dou,' yes?"

Gina had shrugged. "That's a question for the director."

And then she had walked away.

Gina's ambivalence toward her only served to make Dominika more fascinated. She began collecting information on Gina in casual conversation with members of the theater company. She learned that Gina had been offered theater scholarships by every major college drama program in the United States, but had chosen Wellesley. She was Italian-American, from a large well-off family in Connecticut, and her father owned a liquor store. Gina was a senior, like Dominika, and no one knew what Gina would be doing after graduation. Everyone assumed she would go to either Broadway or Hollywood. Her mixture of charisma, beauty, and sexuality made her future stardom a sure bet.

During one late-night rehearsal, Gina and Dominika ran a scene they had played many times before. The line Othello delivered to Desdemona was, "What promise, chuck?" Only this time, when Gina said it, she reached her hand and touched Dominika's cheek as she looked into her eyes.

Dominika felt her body tingle all over. All of her dialogue left her head.

"Dominika?" the director had asked after a pause.

"Um, yes," the Polish girl had replied. "Sorry."

"'I have sent to bid Cassio come speak with you," the director hissed.

"I have sent to bid Cassio come speak with you," Dominika repeated. The tall girl had only revealed her irritation at the end of the scene, shooting a disgusted look at the director as if to say: *Casting this amateur was all your idea.*

Dominika had worked even harder. She studied books on acting, YouTube clips with advice from famous acting coaches, and begged for every tip she could get from the director. Finally the director had taken her aside: "Look, Dom, you're getting way too intense about this."

"I am?"

"Just focus on the character. Okay? Focus on the character and you'll be fine."

"But I want to do well. I do not want to embarrass Gina…"

"You won't. Listen. Gina told me yesterday that you had really improved."

"She did?" Dominika felt an unfamiliar heat creep over her skin.

"Yeah. And God knows how hard it is for me

to impress her, so for you… Well. Just relax. All right? You're doing fine."

Dominika had wondered if the story was true, or if the director only made it up to help her, Dominika, relax. Either way, Dominika decided, if the director thought her relaxing was the best thing for the play, she would try.

Dress rehearsals arrived. The troupe had a sizable wardrobe, and skilled costumers outfitted Dominika in beautiful period dresses, plus one diaphanous nearly see-through nightgown. *If only my parents could see me now,* Dominika thought as she studied her reflection. She smiled. *Dominika, how far you have come!*

Two nights into dress rehearsals, Dominika was trying to lace a bustier in the dressing room. She looked around for assistance, but she was alone. She shrugged. *I'll figure it out,* she thought.

Gina entered, looking preoccupied. With barely a nod to Dominika, she began undressing.

The Polish girl tried not to stare as Gina ripped her t-shirt off and threw it into a corner. The actress's big breasts wobbled in a plain white bra. A couple of movements and her belt was undone. She stepped out of her jeans, leaving them on the floor.

Turning, Gina reached for Othello's military uniform, a mostly black-robe outfit with mushroom shoulders and a deep open V-neck. Then she pulled her hand back again. "Fuck," she muttered. "Undershirt." She turned to Dominika.

"Seen the undershirt?"

The sight of Gina standing in her underwear struck Dominika dumb. The tall Italian-American girl looked spectacular. Her long dark curly hair spilled around her shoulders, and her bra's thin fabric betrayed her aureole—large, light and perfectly round, almost covering her big breast's peaks like caps. Tiny panties could not quite conceal a neatly-trimmed bush. Gina's olive skin was impossibly smooth and creamy. It looked like mocha. For a split-second, Dominika wondered if it tasted like mocha.

"Hey."

"What. Yes. I am listening!"

"Undershirt," Gina said impatiently. "Seen it?"

"No, I'm sorry."

Gina rolled her eyes. She threw on the outfit anyway. Her bra showed through the V-neck. She stormed out toward the stage.

The costumer corrected the undershirt situation minutes later. Dominika was happy for this. She would have been very distracted otherwise.

That night, Dominika lay in bed staring at the ceiling. The light snores of her roommate, a preternaturally nervous Gender Studies major, drifted across the room from where she slept.

Finally, Dominika rose and opened a laptop that rested on her neat desk. She started her web browser, directed it to Google's search page, and typed, "Tribbing." The screen replied:

> Tribadism or *tribbing*, commonly known
> by its scissoring position, is a form of
> non-penetrative sex in which a woman
> rubs her vulva against her partner's body
> for sexual stimulation, especially for
> ample stimulation of the clitoris. This
> may involve female-to-female genital
> contact or a female rubbing her vulva
> against her partner's thigh, stomach,
> buttocks, arm, or other body part
> (excluding the mouth). A variety of sex
> positions are included, including the
> missionary position.

Dominika stared at the text for a long time. Then she closed her browser and returned to bed. After a long pause, she shut her eyes and turned her head to the side. Her hand under the covers moved slowly down her stomach toward the space between her legs.

*   *   *

The next night, at rehearsal, Dominika lay on a table that was standing in for a bed. Gina and the director were arguing about the blocking of the strangulation scene.

"If I'm on the audience side of the bed," Gina said, pointing at the prone Dominika, "they can't see my face or hers when I'm throttling her." She shrugged. "But if I'm on the other side, the audience won't be able to see the dagger when I pull it out beforehand."

"Can't you pull the dagger out, then just walk around?" the director asked.

"Othello wouldn't do that. He's almost crazy at this point. He's going to choose one side or the other without thinking about it. Him changing his mind about what side to approach her would be the last thing he would do."

"Excuse me," Dominika said.

Gina and the director turned. Dominika rarely spoke up.

"Why can Othello not stand at the foot of the bed, withdraw the dagger, and leap at Desdemona on this side"—Dominika indicated her side away from the audience—"and strangle her then?"

After a pause, the director said: "Maybe."

Gina frowned. "If Othello does it that way, he will be really angry. Crazy angry."

Dominika regarded Gina calmly. "Did you not just say he was almost crazy?"

Gina flushed, an unfamiliar sight. "Listen. I know you mean well, but you don't want me to get like that. I don't want to hurt you."

"I think I will be fine." Dominika laced her fingers upon her stomach, completely at ease. "I shall be resisting, after all. Desdemona shall fight for her life." She looked at the director. "No?"

The director shrugged. "It's gonna be really intense if we do it that way." She considered. "But that's maybe not such a bad thing." To

Gina: "How about it?"

Gina glared at Dominika. "Okay, but let's get this straight. If anything goes wrong, or I hurt you, it's on you."

"Of course. It was my idea."

Gina looked at the director. "You're the witness."

The director nodded, then walked away, speaking over her shoulder: "Give it a test run. I'll be back."

Gina approached Dominika, looming over her. "You sure about this?"

Dominika gazed up with her most innocent eyes. "Perhaps I should ask, are YOU sure. I shall be struggling. I will have to place my hands upon you."

The tall girl grinned, the first time she had ever offered her co-star a smile. "I think I can handle it."

"Well then."

Gina placed her hands gently upon Dominika's neck. Up until this point, the experienced actress had not actually touched the blonde girl in this scene. She had always acted the strangulation with her fingers inches from Dominika's throat.

Dominika slipped her hand over Gina's. Her eyelids closed.

"You okay?"

The Polish girl opened her blue eyes. "Yes, I'm ready."

"So we'll just run it through at half speed, and

see how it goes."

"That is fine."

The pressure of Gina's hands did not increase, but the tall girl's body grew tense. Her back curved as she directed her strength into her arms. Gina's face turned angry. Dominika emitted a small cry and slid her hand slowly up Gina's wrist, to her elbow, then to her shoulder. She made a strangled sound.

"Great!"

They turned. The director was behind them, beaming.

"Let's try it with the leap. C'mon!"

Soon, they had blocked out the action. Gina's strong legs lifted her body in a feral bound toward Dominika; Dominika screamed with terror. As Gina's feet hit the boards, her hands flew around the blonde girl's neck. "It is too late!" Gina thundered, the proper line from the play. Dominika thrashed—fighting, writhing, pushing her hands against Gina. She almost fell off the table as she performed her struggles.

"Whoa!" the director said. "Cut!" The action stopped.

The two actors looked around. The entire company was watching, wide-eyed.

The director grinned. "That was pretty good."

"I don't like this," one of the bit players said. "It's violence against women."

The director rolled her eyes.

"What do you want Othello to do, Cindy?"

sneered the makeup girl. "Strangle her with sweet words?"

"I'm just saying, it looks really intense…"

"Good," the director interrupted. "That makes it controversial, and controversy sells tickets. Tweet and Facebook it up about the intensity when you get home, guys. We want a sell-out house on opening night." She beamed at Gina and Dominika. "Nice work, you two! Okay, next scene."

As Gina and the others turned away, Dominika noted to her surprise that the tall girl had barely applied any pressure at all—though the actress's fingers had been rigid and shaking, Gina's grip had been gentle. Dominika touched her throat, feeling where Gina's hands had been. She felt a sudden, fierce tenderness toward Gina, who clearly was concerned for her Polish co-star's welfare.

Two weeks before opening night, full dress and makeup rehearsals began. Dominika received a little powder on her cheeks to help cut down glare from the klieg lights, but otherwise nothing.

"That's all?" she asked the makeup girl.

"That's it," the girl replied. "You don't need much. Makes my job a lot easier. Especially since I have to deal with Othello. Which reminds me, that face paint should've dried by now."

The makeup girl turned and walked toward the dressing room. Dominika followed her.

Inside the room, Dominika saw many of the

cast and crew gathered around Gina, as usual. The Italian-American girl was leaning back in a chair. Makeup had transformed her into an African man. Dominika gasped.

Suzy, the black student who had been the first to see Dominika on the day she had walked through the audition door, grinned at the Polish girl: "Not bad, huh?" Suzy turned to Gina. "'Sup, brotha." She offered her fist. Gina smiled and bumped it with her own.

Annabelle entered. The happy vibe in the room vanished immediately.

"You all look so charming!" she announced, faking a broad smile. With her finger, she indicated Gina. "I'm sorry, but could we just have a quick moment?"

Everyone but Gina filed out. The tall girl's expression was blank. She stared at the wall in front of her. Annabelle nodded and smiled to the theater girls as they left, then closed the door behind them.

Outside, everyone dispersed quickly as if they had pressing business. Everyone except for Dominika. She lingered, and soon heard raised voices from inside.

"… Put up with this any longer," Annabelle screeched.

"Do we really have to do this here?" Gina replied. "What the hell? You'll have me all to yourself for the rest of the night after rehearsal. Can't you wait a couple hours?"

"That's exactly the problem," Gina's girlfriend replied. Dominika imagined her drawing herself up and looking down at Gina with those cold eyes. "You're all about wait, wait, wait! Well, I'm tired of waiting. What are we doing after graduation?"

"We've been over this…"

"Yes, and your plan seems to be minimum-wage employment doing summer stock in whatever farm town that will take you. If they'll take you. Guess what. I'm not going to be driving to work, earning a living, and supporting you while you go off and have your fun. I don't have the luxury of coming from a rich family."

"Oh, my God." A tone of weariness, of being beaten down, crept into Gina's voice. "Let's not get into this again…"

"And what? Just wait? Keep waiting? Right, that's always your plan. Let me tell you this for the millionth time, and maybe it will sink in. Unlike you, I will have student debt to pay. Unlike you, I want a sound financial future—one that I've earned MYSELF. I've lined up a very good job in Dallas doing investment auditing. I'm happy to pay the rent, like I said, but I will not be sitting around like a chump while you go off on auditions and tours and who the fuck knows what. You need to be home with me. It is time to be an adult, Gina. This is real life, and this is what adults do."

A long pause followed. Annabelle spoke again.

"So I am asking you, right here, right now: are you ready to grow up?"

A longer silence.

"You are so selfish," Annabelle said. Her sobs carried through in her voice. "You are the most selfish person I have ever known."

It took all of Dominika's restraint not to burst through the door and attack Annabelle. *How dare you?* the Polish girl seethed. *Someone with Gina's gifts? You want her to stay home and be your fucking HOUSEWIFE?* Dominika gasped as she realized her language, in her head at least, was so vituperative. She had never once uttered the F-word in her life.

Annabelle stormed out of the dressing room, slamming the door so hard the walls shivered. She marched toward the exit, away from Dominika.

After many seconds had passed, Dominika rapped the smallest of knocks with her little-finger knuckle. "Hello?" she asked softly. "May I come in?"

No reply. She hesitated, then turned the knob.

Gina was sitting in her chair staring at the wall. An emptiness was in her eyes.

"Hello," the blonde said, for lack of anything else.

"Hello."

Dominika wanted so badly to hug her.

The director poked her head into the room, knocking on the door as softly as Dominika had.

"Need a few minutes?"

"For what?" Gina rose to her feet. She seemed calm. "Work calls, right?"

Gina performed as brilliantly in rehearsal as she always did.

The following week, opening night arrived. Dominika strode up and down the corridor backstage, fighting a case of the butterflies.

"Do me a favor," the stage manager told her. "Go pace somewhere else. Please? I'm nervous enough and with my blood pressure the way it feels tonight, you're about to send me to the emergency room."

Dominika walked away and around, toward the stage. The audience on the other side murmured a dull roar, like water rushing down a steep river.

The Polish girl approached Gina and the director, who were peeking through the red velvet curtain at the crowd.

"Full house," Gina said. "You got what you wanted."

"I'm kind of wishing I could take it back. We had to turn people away. I don't remember the last time that happened." The director paused, then asked in a casual tone: "Do you see her?"

"No," Gina replied. She shrugged her shoulders, and her costume rippled with the movement. "She promised she would come, even so, but breaking promises is kind of her thing."

"What do you mean?" The director turned to

look at Gina. "'Even so?'"

"We broke up Wednesday," the tall girl replied calmly.

The director said nothing.

The brunette kept looking out through the curtain. "I guess it's for the best. Who knows. I don't care."

The director tentatively reached a hand toward Gina's arm, hesitated, then drew it back again. "I'm really sorry."

"It happens."

"You gonna be okay?"

"I'll be fine. I won't let it affect my performance."

"That's not what I meant—"

"Yeah, I know. Thanks. I'm fine. Really."

Dominika turned around and walked toward the backstage area again, her brain spinning.

After the curtain had opened and Iago and Roderigo were strolling the boards speaking the opening lines, Dominika approached the director.

"What is it, Dom?" the director whispered. She was focused on the action.

"I'm sorry, but what is my first line?" the blonde whispered back.

The director turned to her, bug-eyed. "Please tell me you're kidding."

Dominika said nothing.

"'My noble father, I do perceive here a divided duty.'"

"Right," the Polish girl said. "Right. I've got it

now. Don't worry."

The director kept staring.

Dominika's first scene arrived. She played it perfectly. Kneeling by Othello, she kept her eyes on the floor and spoke:

"…And to his honor and his valiant parts

"Did I my soul and fortunes consecrate.

"So that, dear lords, if I be left behind,

"A moth of peace, and he go to the war,

"The rites for which I love him are bereft me,

"And I a heavy interim shall support

"By his dear absence. Let me go with him."

She looked up at Gina.

Later, at the beginning of the strangulation scene, Dominika tried to focus on her lines and not on Gina. The tall girl trembled with rage, her eyes shining wildly. In the script faithful Desdemona had just unwittingly made her husband Othello think she had been unfaithful; and, not comprehending his anger, Desdemona had become more and more afraid. On her bed (a twin-size purloined temporarily from a dorm room), Dominika snapped upright per the rehearsals, but suddenly realized to her mortification that her nipples had turned into pebbles and must be creating what Americans called "headlights" through the gauzy material of her nightdress. She withstood the temptation to look down and see, and instead cried her line:

"Kill me to-morrow: let me live to-night!"

"Nay, if you strive—"

"But half an hour!" Dominika wailed.

"Being done, there is no pause," Gina uttered ominously.

"But while I say one prayer!"

Gina leapt. Her hands flew around Dominika's throat; Dominika grabbed Gina's sleeves and thrashed. In her contortions, the Polish girl's breast brushed Gina's arm, something that had never happened before. Dominika felt electricity sizzle through her body, stunning her; gasping, her eyes snapped open. She writhed an uncontrollable, wrenching jerk.

The bed capsized, toppling Dominika and Gina with it over and onto the stage boards and almost into the front row. This also had never happened before. Gina did not miss a beat; she kept her hands on Dominika's neck and thrust her body upon the Polish girl's, between her legs. "It is too late!" Gina screamed with a feral hatred.

The audience gasped; many jumped to their feet, ready to storm the stage or run for help. "Down!" screamed young women in the back seats. "Sit down, goddamn it!" The audience stood up en masse. They watched Dominika's struggles gradually subside; Gina withdrew her hands. On cue, Dominika uttered a tiny sob.

"What noise is this? Not dead? Not yet quite dead?" Gina whispered. "I that am cruel am yet merciful; I would not have thee linger in thy pain: So, so." Gina and Dominika performed the choreographed action where Othello snapped

Desdemona's neck. Dominika jerked, then moved no more. The audience gasped again.

And then Gina went off script. She began to weep. A small sniffling at first, then a gasping, sobbing, uncontrollable grief.

The audience watched, unblinking. Gina cried so hard that snot ran out of her nose. Dominika, lying motionless, wondered: *What is happening?* It took all of her self-control not to look. *Is Gina crying because it's good for the play? Is her grief because of Annabelle leaving her? Did perhaps Gina worry that she has hurt me?*

The girl playing Emilia shouted off-stage, "O, good my lord, I would speak a word with you!"

Gina did not respond, keening. Emilia hesitated, and then screamed at the top of her lungs: "My good lord, I would speak a word with you!" After a moment, Gina rose, wiped her face, and spoke the next line.

At the curtain calls, the cast and crew repeatedly bowed, walked off, and then strode back in front of the applauding ticketholders. The audience would not stop clapping.

"This is nuts," said the girl who had played Iago. She beamed, glowing.

Gina turned to Dominika. "Did I hurt you?"

Dominika offered a warm, radiant smile. "No. Your hands were as gentle as ever."

"Cool." Gina turned away.

Cool? That's all? Dominika tried to keep a smile on her face when they trooped out onto the stage again for their umpteenth bow.

The play sold out for the rest of its two-week run. After much discussion, the troupe agreed that the bed falling over was a terrific touch. Gina and Dominika kept re-playing it to perfection.

Near the end of the run, the director ran in waving her smartphone as the cast and crew arrived for the night's show.

"Motherfucker!" she breathed. "I only just found out about this. Gather around, everybody! We got a review from the goddamn Boston Globe!"

The girls all clustered round. "And I quote," the director intoned. She tapped her phone, and began scrolling through text: "'It is not often that a drama critic works for free; however, when one has a daughter at Wellesley, and one is visiting said daughter for the weekend, and said daughter insists on attending an opening night show because of buzz on this new thing called "the internet," well, what is a father to do?'" The reviewer went on to describe the production overall in glowing terms.

Then: "'But it is the young lady in the lead, Gina Mantovani, who steals this already considerable show. In my twenty years of reviewing theater, I have never seen a better Othello; indeed, and I say this seriously, I may never have seen a better actor.'" The crowd around the director gasped. Gina, trying to break the tension, remarked: "Wait. I'm not an actress?

Somebody call this guy."

"Shh," the director said to Gina. She continued reading: "Mantovani's range, depth of emotion, gift of craft, and yes I must say this (as a happily married man, I hasten to add), smoldering sexuality makes her the top pick for future international stardom, if there were such a fantasy league devoted to such matters. I, and soon many more I am sure, look forward to seeing her work again."

A pause. "That's it," the director said. Everyone looked at Gina.

The girl smiled, bent her head, and rubbed the back of her neck. "Wow."

"That's all you can say?" someone asked.

The director turned her phone's screen to Gina, so that she could read the text. "With this review, you can get auditions on Broadway. For real."

"Just remember all us little people, okay?" another girl joked.

Gina smiled again, nodded, and made a self-effacing remark. At length, the company broke up to put on that night's production, which was a smash as usual.

Long after the show was over and everyone else had departed, Dominika sat in the dressing room, still in her stage nightgown. She felt that a very precious time in her life was drawing to a close, and she wanted to linger and remember.

"Oh. Hey. I thought everybody had gone," she

heard behind her.

Rising to her feet and turning, she saw Gina in the doorway dressed in her regular t-shirt and jeans. The tall girl grinned. "Forgot my homework." Entering, she picked up a backpack and slid it upon her shoulders.

Dominika said nothing. She was aware of her hair down, of the nightdress upon her body, of how little the garment left to the imagination. She wondered if Gina cared.

It seemed she didn't. Gina turned to leave. But then she paused, and turned back to the blonde girl. Dominika felt her skin grow hot under Gina's gaze.

"That strangulation scene made the play," Gina said finally. "And that was because of you. So I wouldn't have gotten that review if it wasn't for you. So, thanks." Before Dominika could reply, the actress had disappeared.

Dominika cursed herself. *That was your moment,* she thought. *Your big moment. And what did you say? Nothing!* However, even in her frustration, Dominika admitted that she did not know what, exactly, she could have said because she did not know what, exactly, she wanted.

After the final performance and the last curtain call, many tears were shed backstage.

"It isn't over yet!" Gina announced. She held up her hands. "Wrap party is tomorrow, my place. There will be plenty of alcohol—compliments of my dad, and his liquor store."

Cheers. "He and my mom are not leaving until morning, otherwise we could just have the shindig tonight. So anyway, head over to my dorm tomorrow. Party starts at noon, and ends when everybody is either passed out or expelled." Whoops and high-fives all around.

As everyone began to leave, Dominika wanted to say something to Gina. But she did not know what. So, she asked the tall girl if it would be all right if she, Dominika, brought along a few of her Widows a cappella singing friends. Gina assured her that that would be more than fine, and made sure Dominika knew where to go.

The Polish girl and her Widows friends arrived at the party early evening. Dominika was surprised to see that almost all of the cast and crew were already there. When Gina had said the party began at noon, Dominika had thought she was kidding.

"Desdemona!" Gina cried, throwing open the door. She clearly had had quite a bit to drink. "I greet thee… well, shit, I can't remember any Shakespeare but anyway, come on in!"

Dominika had the great pleasure of introducing her Widows singing friends to Gina and her theater friends. *Who would have thought,* she reflected, *that the shy Polish girl would one day have such a social network?* She felt a proud glow of accomplishment. And then, suddenly, she remembered that she had not achieved all she desired.

Before the party, Dominika had stood naked in her bathroom, studying her body in the mirror. *How do I accomplish this?* she had wondered. The problem was that she still did not know, exactly, what she wanted from Gina. All she knew was that Gina had been constantly in her thoughts, almost from the moment she had met her.

Do I want to be her lover? Dominika felt her cheeks burn, both for her thoughts about sex and for embarrassment at her own vacillation. She felt like Hamlet, a character whose biography she had read when researching Shakespeare generally for her acting. *What do I want?* She did not even know if Gina was attracted to her, or could be attracted to her. The blonde took a deep breath, and closed her eyes. *You must calm yourself,* she thought. *Focus, and approach this rationally.*

She opened her eyes. Looking down, she stared at her bush, a thin triangle of pubic hair so blonde and fine that it was almost invisible. She ran her fingertips through the thatch absently. *I am very blonde, it is true,* she reflected. Gina's ex-girlfriend, Annabelle, was also blonde. *That is something in my favor.* Yes, it was in her favor if Dominika wanted to be Gina's lover. But did she?

Dominika kept gazing downward. She felt paralyzed. She burned with emotions for Gina, and, yes, felt a sexual hunger for Gina, a hunger that she had never felt for another person. But Dominika's experience with sex was non-existent, and even if she desired a sexual experience (*or, could it be hoped, experiences, plural!*) with the tall Italian-American goddess, the outcome would most likely be disastrous. And then their friendship, tentative as it was, would be destroyed. Gina would want nothing to do with her ever again.

And even if such a physical relationship somehow were successful, what of the future? It was obvious that Gina would follow a stage career, perhaps in New York. Dominika would be returning to Europe after graduation, in only a few short weeks. She had been accepted to the best medical school in Poland, located in Kraków. It was all arranged. A "done deal," as the Americans said. Dear Americans! She would miss them.

And she would miss Gina most of all. The thought tightened her throat. She fought the urge to cry. For a wild moment, Dominika fantasized about Gina joining her in Kraków, learning Polish and becoming the toast of Poland's acting world. But she knew that that would never happen.

Dominika sighed. She had gotten no further than where she had been before. What did she want with Gina? From Gina? The blonde stared hard at her naked reflection in the mirror. The girl who stared back was petite, pale, and perhaps sexy. Was a one-night stand, a "hookup," really the best that she could realistically expect for herself and Gina, given their circumstances? Perhaps so.

Dominika tried not to think about how hard it would be to leave Gina in the morning after such an encounter. She took one last deep breath, nodded, turned off the bathroom light and entered her bedroom to dress.

At the party, everything had gone wrong. Gina was constantly surrounded by well-wishers and friends; her charisma attracted people like a bulb attracts moths. Dominika had only found one opportunity to exchange a few words with the tall girl. Gina was constantly on the move, thanking people for their congratulations and attending to hostess duties.

And now Gina's roommate Tracy had begun the Linda Lovelace challenge, of which Gina was good-humoredly taking part. The participating young women sat on the floor cross-legged in a circle, egged on by the tipsy cheers of their peers. Dominika watched one girl fit a whole eight inches of zucchini down her throat. *A blow job.* That is what they were called. The Polish girl had difficulty believing that men and women actually did such things. If she, Dominika, ever married, would her husband expect her to swallow his… phallus? The thought nauseated her. She looked around for a distraction. Dominika watched the TV weatherman issue grim warnings of an imminent cold front.

The zucchini passed to the next girl: Gina. The noise in the room rose an octave. Dominika glanced. Gina held the vegetable and smirked at it. Then she wiped it on her shirt with a long, slow, sexy twisting motion, in and out. The onlookers howled.

"Where'd she learn to do that!" one of her friends shouted.

"Drama school!"

"Must've been some teacher!"

"How do I get that teacher!"

Gina glanced at her onlookers saucily. Then she raised the zucchini and began to slide it, slowly, into her mouth. The girls counted off the inch marks: "One!… Two!… Three!…"

It kept disappearing… and disappearing. The cries became higher-pitched as Gina broke the eight-inch record and still kept going. "Ten!… Eleven!… Twelve! THIRTEEN! FOURTEEN!"

Gina had slid the zucchini as far down into her throat as it could go. She smiled, and slowly withdrew it.

Dominika watched, fascinated. She realized that she had risen out of her chair and joined the throng, getting herself a front-row seat as it were. *Why am I not thinking very clearly?* she wondered. Dominika glanced down at a plastic cup in her hand. It held an icy red liquid. *Ah yes,* she thought. *Strawberry margaritas.* How many had she drank? She had lost count after three. And she intended to drink many more. If she could not talk to Gina, at least she could get herself passed-out drunk.

Girls were asking Gina, some seriously, about

her swallowing secret. Gina grinned. "It's all in the wrist."

"I ain't following that act," said the girl who received the zucchini next.

Suddenly the door flew open. "So here's a party. I might have known!"

Annabelle was dressed to the nines as usual. She walked in, offering little waves as if she were on the red carpet at the Oscars. "Hello everybody! Oh, are we late? Ha, ha!" Annabelle swayed slightly; clearly she had had a few, herself.

The noise in the room died. Only the stereo, playing hip-hop, could be heard. Someone shut it off.

"Hey! No music? Aw, c'mon. Mike likes music. Where is he. Mike!" Annabelle turned around, looking.

A preppy young man entered, ill at ease. He shut the door behind him.

"Heeere he is," Annabelle trilled. "Everybody: meet Mike! He's at Harvard. And he is awesome."

Gina rose from the floor. The other sitting girls did the same, looking down. Gina walked away. She turned up a flight of stairs, disappearing from view.

"Not leaving 'cause of lil' ol' me, are you?" Annabelle called after Gina. Upstairs, a door slammed. Annabelle shrugged. "Well, that's a shame. I wanted you to meet Mike."

"Uh… what's happening here?" Mike whispered to Annabelle.

"Nothing! I just wanted you to meet some acquaintances. Wanted to show you off. Because you, my friend…" Annabelle paused, and leaned all the way over so that she could shout up the stairwell: "Are somebody with a FUTURE!"

"Fuck off," Dominika heard herself utter.

A pin's drop could have been heard. Annabelle's head slowly swiveled around. Her cold eyes settled ominously upon Dominika. "What did you say?"

"I said fuck off. Nobody wants you here. FUCK OFF!" Dominika hurled her drink, cup and all, into Annabelle's face. The victim gasped; red liquid dribbled down onto her expensive white sweater. Dominika kicked Annabelle in the shin with all her strength. The Hitchcock blonde cried out, clutched her leg, and toppled over like a tree. Dominika kicked her again, and would have lunged upon her but was restrained by the guests.

Mike backed away. "I don't know what's going on here," he said. "But I'm out." He turned, opened the door, and exited.

"No!" Annabelle raised herself, hobbling after him. "Wait! Wait! Don't go!" She cast a frightened look back at Dominika, who was spewing obscenities and struggling to get at Annabelle through the many arms that held her back. Annabelle hurried out the door. Somebody closed it.

In moments, Gina reappeared, wide-eyed. "What happened?" she asked. "Was there a fight?"

People explained what had gone down.

"Where's Dominika?"

All heads turned toward the corner.

The Polish girl sat sobbing in her chair, head cradled on her knees. In contrast to her formidable display earlier, she now seemed very small and fragile.

Gina approached. "Hey," she said. "Hey."

Dominika gave no sign of having heard. She kept crying.

"Hey," Gina repeated for the third time. She placed an awkward hand upon the blonde's shoulder. "You all right?"

"I'm sorry," Dominika said through her sobs.

"Sorry for what? You just did what my roommate has said she's always wanted to do." Gina glanced at Tracy, who nodded grimly.

"You just became my new best friend," Tracy said.

Dominika made no reply, only weeping louder.

The guests shuffled their feet. "You know, it's getting late," someone said.

"Yeah…"

"No!" Gina jumped up. "What? Annabelle gets her ass kicked, and everyone's depressed?"

A few girls laughed.

"C'mon," the Italian-American continued. She brushed her long black curly hair over her shoulders. "This is a happy occasion. All right? Let's not let Annabelle ruin the party." Gina turned back to Dominika, kneeling and patting her knee. "Okay?" she asked softly.

Tracy turned the music back on. People began chatting again.

When Dominika finally looked up, she saw Gina, still kneeling and looking at her.

"Hey," Gina said.

"Hey."

"That was some beatdown. So I heard. You couldn't have waited till I was around?"

Dominika coughed a laugh and wiped her nose.

"Are all Polish girls as tough as you?"

"No," Dominika said seriously. "And I am not tough."

Gina considered her. "Yeah. Right."

"I should leave." Dominika made to rise.

"No!" Gina pushed her back into the chair with a gentle hand. "You're not going anywhere."

"Why not?"

"Because I have to go get some more chips and stuff." Gina glanced at empty bowls on the counters and tables. "And I'll need some help bringing everything back. What do you say? Come with. Okay?"

Dominika looked down. After a moment, she nodded.

"Good." Gina rose and spoke a quick word to Tracy. Then she beckoned.

As Gina and Dominika left the apartment, they shivered. "Wow," the taller girl gasped. "It's freezing."

"The television said that a cold front was approaching," Dominika said as they hurried down steps to the sidewalk.

"Approaching, my ass. It's here." She glanced at the blonde. "Did you bring a coat?"

"No."

"Want one?"

Dominika shook her head.

"Okay. Well, we better jog."

They broke into a trot. Dominika followed Gina's lead. They crossed the campus, taking many short cuts.

On a sprint across a field, Dominika slipped and fell. "Ow!" She rolled on the grass, clutching her ankle.

Gina was immediately kneeling by her side. "Oh, shit. Okay, let's see." Gina examined the ankle, asking where it hurt.

Dominika realized that their faces were very close together. She liked the feel of Gina's warm hands on her ankles and legs.

With a start, the blonde realized Gina was saying something. "What? Sorry."

"I said, can you stand?"

The taller girl helped her to her feet. Dominika tried putting a little weight on her injured ankle. She grimaced, lifted it, and hopped on the other foot.

"Okay, clearly, that's not gonna work. We…" Gina's voice trailed off.

Puzzled, Dominika studied her.

Gina was staring at her companion's chest.

Following the tall girl's gaze, Dominika looked straight down. The cold wind had made Dominika's nipples hard. Her white shirt had pressed close to her breasts like a second skin. Her bra and what it contained were clearly visible through the perspiration-wet fabric.

"Sorry," Gina said.

"That's all right."

"So," the Italian-American continued, all business. "You hopping isn't gonna cut it. We need to get there and back, fast. If I'd known this weather would have picked up, I wouldn't have left at all." She glanced at approaching dark clouds. "Let me carry you piggyback."

"Piggy what?"

"Just hop on." Gina squatted in front of her. After Dominika's protests came to naught, she climbed onto Gina's back. The taller girl lifted her effortlessly and resumed running toward the blinking lights of the campus sundry store.

"You are very strong," Gina said.

"Yeah, well. Say. Those are some headlights you got there."

Dominika glanced down. Her bouncing breasts were rubbing against Gina's back.

Dominika giggled. "This happens on certain occasions."

"Yeah. Like plays."

"What?"

"You're lucky I didn't forget my lines on opening night."

Dominika was struck dumb. She thought Gina had not noticed her headlights during the strangulation scene.

"It was everything I could do to not... Okay, we're here." Gina slowed. A sign on the front door of the shop read: "COLD FRONT COMING. STAY INSIDE. THIS MEANS YOU!"

"Bitches!" Gina exclaimed. "They mean, THEY will go stay inside. Shit. Okay. Well, that was a wasted trip."

Not at all, Dominika thought as Gina turned back, jogging along a street. The Polish girl snuggled close, wrapping her arms around the brunette. Her arms accidentally brushed the bottom of Gina's big breasts.

"Careful," Gina warned.

"Sorry."

"No, it's not that. If you distract me too much, I may get lost and we'll freeze out here."

Dominika laughed, and Gina laughed with her. They talked happily about the play, enjoying a feeling of closeness that had eluded them before.

"Hey, I'm gonna cut next to the pond by the road. We'll get home faster. Okay?"

"Lead on, MacDuff!"

"Wrong play!"

Gina dived through some trees. In seconds, her legs were pumping by the pond's muddy bank.

Dominika felt the tall girl's feet slip. "Uh oh," Gina said.

The next thing Dominika knew, she was sitting in shallow water and covered in mud.

"Dominika!" The Italian-American crawled up fast. "Are you okay?"

"Yes," the blonde replied, slightly dazed. "I believe so."

"God, I'm sorry." Furious, Gina smacked her fist into her thigh, hard. "I get you out and twist your ankle, now this. What's next. Hypothermia?"

As if in response, a terribly cold wind ripped through them. The girls shrieked.

"Oh, the water feels so warm!" Dominika gasped. She turned and moved toward the middle of the pond, frog-paddling.

Gina began to tell her not to, but the Polish girl was laughing. Gina watched blonde hair disappear under the water and then pop up again.

"In Europe we swim in natural water," Dominika said. "Like this. It is good for the body." She laughed again, ecstatic.

"Girl, you are truly something else." Gina hesitated, then dove in to join her. She surfaced next to Dominika.

"Is this not so much better?" Dominika said.

"Yeah," Gina replied, spitting water. "But we can't stay here all night."

"Will you keep me warm?" Before the brunette could answer, the Polish girl embraced her, holding her close. After a moment, she also wrapped her legs around the taller girl's waist.

Gina treaded water until she found a spot where she could stand on firm bottom with their heads above the surface. She held Dominika tenderly. The blonde closed her eyes and set her face on Gina's shoulder. "You were always so gentle," she whispered. "In the play. You never bruised me, not even one time."

"I'm glad," Gina replied. "I was really worried about that. Like, it kept me up nights. You know?"

"You did not seem worried."

"I know. A lot of reasons for that."

They said nothing more. Dominika moved her hands slowly up and down Gina's back, feeling her warmth and strength. Gina closed her eyes. After a moment she added: "I take it back. Maybe we can stay here all night."

In response, Dominika tightened her legs around the taller girl. She felt Gina breathe harder. Their cheeks were touching. Slowly, they slid their faces toward each other, their lips growing closer…

"Hey!"

Startled, they both jumped as their heads turned. It was a portly security guard in a heavy coat. He had a remarkable resemblance to Don King. Trudging toward them from the road through the grass, he bellowed: "What the hell are you doing!"

The girls disentangled themselves. "Nothing officer," Gina shouted.

"Yeah, well." The uniformed man paused at the pond's bank, eyeing them doubtfully. "Y'all students here?"

"Yes."

"Okay. Well, listen. If it was up to me, I'd let you canoodle all night because your business ain't mine. But I'm under orders. All people, all, need to get inside, right now. There's hail coming."

"Hail?" Dominika asked. She shivered.

"That's right. And that ain't all. Some freezing rain, and all kinds of nice surprises. The longer you ladies stay in here, the tougher it'll be when you get out. This pond might well freeze over by morning."

"We're leaving now, officer." Gina strode out of the water, helping Dominika as she hopped on one foot.

"You need a ride?" the security officer asked. "Shouldn't be walking around soaked in this cold."

Gina looked at Dominika, then back at the portly man. "That would be great."

Soon, the man's campus security car was depositing the girls outside of Gina's dorm. "Sorry we got your seats wet," Gina called as they stepped out of the back seat.

"Ain't my cleaning bill," the officer said. "Y'all go on and get inside now. Warm up!"

The girls closed the car door, waved, and ran

inside. The car rolled away.

"Hot shower, hot shower," Dominika chanted in a mantra as she hopped shivering up the stairs with Gina's help.

"You got it," Gina said.

Inside, the party guests gaped as Gina and Dominika entered. The girls left a trail of dripping water on the carpet.

"Yo, where are the chips?" a girl asked.

Gina gave her a look.

"Kidding. Seriously, what happened?"

"Tell you later." Gina turned to Dominika. "You gonna be okay getting up the stairs?"

"Yes." The blonde girl gripped the banister and hopped up the carpeted steps, one by one. She heard Gina ask, "Where's the whiskey? Really yo, I need to warm up."

Dominika reached the upper floor. "Which bathroom should I use?" she called down.

"First door on your right," a voice shouted up at her. "There's only one bathroom in this place."

Dominika saw the door, slightly ajar. She pushed it. The bathroom was empty. She stumbled inside, shivering. Locking the door behind her, she leaned against the washbasin and began removing her sopping clothes.

A soft knock came from the door. Dominika jumped. "Who is it?"

"Me." Gina.

"Oh. Hello."

The handle rattled.

Dominika reached over and unlocked it without thinking.

"Hey," Gina said, slipping inside. She re-locked the door behind her.

"Hey."

"You okay?"

"What? Oh. Yes, I think so."

"Good. Let's go." Gina started to strip. Her soggy shirt made a *splissshhh* sound as it hit the linoleum floor.

Dominika's jaw dropped. "Go? Go where?"

"Into the shower, where else? We're both freezing and there's not much hot water. Our water heater's the size of a thermos." Holding onto the wall towel rack for balance, Gina removed her socks, the last item of clothing on her body.

Dominika's brain reeled. She realized that the object of her dreams and fantasies was standing stark naked in front of her. She was RIGHT THERE.

Gina, however, seemed all business once again. She turned on the tub taps and pulled the faucet's plunger up to direct the water to the showerhead. Her big breasts wobbled as she moved, bent at the waist. Glancing back, she frowned. "What's up?"

"Eh?"

"I'm telling you, this water will go from hot to cold in nothing flat. If you're coming in, let's go. You look like you're freezing."

Dominika undressed as quickly as she could, on autopilot. Her mind felt numb. She would be naked with Gina… What did that mean? Was Gina only wanting to shower as a pretext for them doing something sexual? Dominika decided that she did not care if that actually was the case. And, anyway, she was indeed freezing. With two yanks, she removed her own socks and then stood as naked as her host.

"Come on," Gina said. Placing a gentle arm around the smaller girl, she helped the blonde hop over to the shower. "You get in first. Hold onto the wall handle there, above the soap dish. You don't want to fall. You've been through enough tonight."

She is so tender, Dominika thought. A wave of powerful emotions rushed through her, and she fought to keep her voice steady. "Thank you."

"No prob. You good? Okay. Here I come." Gina stepped into the tub with her and pulled the shower curtain closed.

Dominika stood closer to the showerhead. Gina directed the jets high, so that water rained onto both of them.

"Aaaaah," Dominika moaned. The air began to steam. "That feels so good. Hot water!"

"Enjoy it while you can," Gina said.

Dominika opened her eyes. Gina was shampooing her hair, grimacing as she squeezed her eyelids shut to keep the soap out.

Dominika stared. The Italian-American's big

breasts were impossibly firm, jiggling as she scrubbed her scalp. Gina had trimmed her pubic hair into a perfect triangle, a patch of mystery between her creamy olive-skinned thighs. Water rivulets ran down her body exquisitely. Dominika stared at Gina's breasts again, almost eye-level; *if I reach my tongue just a little bit…* The Polish girl was sorely tempted. But she was too shy; and, anyway, she did not want to startle her host, whose eyes remained shut.

Gina rinsed her tresses, twisting out the dark locks behind her head. Her eyelids opened. She smiled. "Hi."

"Hi," Dominika replied. Gina was so beautiful. The blonde felt shy, inadequate, and horny, all at once. Horny! *Yes, I do,* she thought. *Who would not, with this amazing girl?*

"You have mud in your hair," Gina said. She touched Dominika's head.

Dominika felt the same jolt of electricity through her body that she had experienced in early rehearsals, when the actress had touched her cheek. "What?"

"Mud." Gina withdrew a finger and held it up. "See?" A little bit of dirt disappeared under the jets.

"Oh. Yes."

"Here, let me." Gina squirted shampoo onto one of her palms and began lathering Dominika's scalp.

Instinctively, Dominika placed her hands on

Gina's hips for balance, bowing her head and closing her eyes. They stood so close that the Polish girl could feel Gina's breath on her hair.

"Isn't that better?" the brunette whispered. She rinsed out the blonde tresses, running her fingers through them slowly and luxuriously, as if it was something she had long wanted to do.

In response, Dominika snuggled in close. Her arms snaked around the taller girl, and she turned her head so that her ear rested against Gina's chest between her big breasts. She felt Gina inhale sharply. Dominika listened to Gina's heart race at a breakneck tempo, betraying the brunette's excitement.

The water grew progressively colder as the water heater failed. Gina's hands rubbed the smaller girl's back, massaging, warming her. The hands moved lower, then lower still. They finally slid over Dominika's tight round ass before holding it. The Polish girl squeezed Gina closer.

A bang at the door startled them. They separated, looking at the entrance.

"Yo!" a drunken girl cried from the hall. Another bang. "How long you gonna be in there? I gotta pee!"

Gina exhaled: a long, loud noise of frustration. Dominika said nothing, but felt the same way.

"Yo!" the voice repeated. The girl outside began rapping on the door with her fist. "I'm serious, bitches, I'm gonna let go right here on your carpet. I been holding it as long as I can…"

"Okay, okay!" Gina shouted. She stepped out of the tub. "We're coming."

"'We?' How many you got in there!" The tipsy girl laughed.

Gina retrieved a folded towel from under the sink and tossed it to Dominika. The blonde turned off the water, stepped out of the tub, and quickly dried herself.

The waiting girl began moaning her discomfort. Gina wrapped her own towel around herself; it barely covered her torso. Dominika followed suit. Gina opened the door.

"Fuuuck, dude, just in time," the drunk guest mumbled, stumbling in. She dropped her pants before she had even reached the toilet. Gina exited, gesturing at Dominika to follow.

The couple left the bathroom and walked down the hall. Gina led Dominika into a dark room. She closed the door behind her and switched on the light. Two twin beds; Tracy and Gina's bedroom. The beds were pushed against opposite walls, showing a clear demarcation— Tracy's half was strewn with clothes, books and detritus, while Gina's half displayed an almost obsessive tidiness.

Dominika gazed at pictures that Gina had taped over her bed. The Italian-American smiled and posed with dark-haired people who looked like her—family members. A few holes in the picture collage on the wall puzzled Dominika, until she remembered: Annabelle. Gina had removed all of her ex's photos.

The Polish girl glanced further and froze. The color drained from her face.

Gina, who had been watching her, gaped with alarm. "What is it? What's wrong?"

The tall girl followed her gaze. On Gina's spotless desk next to her bed lay a black strapon, the phallus so shiny that it displayed reflections on its surface.

"Oh. Oh, shit," Gina gasped. She looked around wildly, then whipped off her towel to throw over the strapon. She turned to Dominika. "I'm sorry—"

Dominika stepped back from the naked girl.

"No!" Gina cried. She struggled to keep her voice steady. "Just wait two seconds, okay? I can explain. Wait."

The brunette hurried to her closet, her hourglass figure jiggling. She withdrew a terrycloth robe and donned it, tying the belt around her waist. "Listen," she said, giving Dominika a beseeching look. "Yes, okay, that's mine. I bought it. But I bought it a long time ago."

"Do you always leave it out there?" the Polish girl whispered. Her color had not yet returned to her face.

"Of course not." Gina sighed. "All right. This is, well, kind of awkward but it's the whole truth. And you deserve the whole truth." After a pause, Gina continued:

"I got that... on a trip with Annabelle. Dominika, please, look at me. We were on a vacation, and she wanted to go to a sex shop, and... The strapon wasn't exactly her idea, I admit, it was both our idea. She said she wanted to try it, she wanted... Anyway, when we got home she changed her mind. And I couldn't return it. I had been the one who paid for it, naturally." Gina shook her head. "So it just stayed in a box under my bed. It's never been used. Not once."

"And so why was it there? Out?"

Gina looked at her feet. "I got it out earlier, when Annabelle came with that guy. I figured she'd come up to my room with him, being all, 'Hey, look at my new BOYfriend.' I wanted it to be like, when they walked in, he would see it and think, oh, okay, so this girl I'm dating used to get it from this other girl, who maybe was bigger than me." Gina looked up. "I wanted to embarrass her."

"Oh."

"I'm not proud of myself. I admit it."

"I see."

"So then I heard the fight downstairs—you, and her. And I rushed out and forgot all about it, till now."

Dominika exhaled. "I thought perhaps... you had left it out for me. That you had planned all this—"

"No!"

"I know now; I believe you."

"I would never... I would never, ever."

"Yes. I believe you."

"You don't know how much I..."

Dominika waited. Gina's voice trailed off. She looked down again.

Downstairs, the music stopped.

"I think the party's ending," Gina said. She returned to her closet, and withdrew another robe. She handed it to Dominika.

The blonde girl laughed, a happy sound breaking the tension. "This... is too big for me." And it was. The bathrobe was Gina's size. Dominika's feet would have tripped over the dragging hem.

Gina frowned. "Oh... right." She looked in the closet again. "How about this?"

Minutes later the girls descended the carpeted steps to the first floor, Gina in her robe, Dominika in pajamas whose pant and wrist cuffs had been rolled up high.

"How's it going?" Gina asked her roommate Tracy.

Tracy shrugged. "Everybody's out. This is getting ugly." She nodded at the window. Wind thrashed the trees. "Forecast says hail will start any second, so it's exodus time."

The guests called their goodbyes to Gina and Tracy, and Dominika too, as they left through the door.

"I'm out too," Tracy continued. "Daniel

called."

"Aw, no," Gina said. "You're driving? In this weather?"

Tracy smirked. "He promised me hot chocolate. And maybe other things." She extended her hand to Dominika. "It was really nice meeting you."

The Polish girl shook hands. "You too."

Tracy smiled. "I meant it when I said you're my new best friend. Take care of her, okay?" Tracy shot Gina a knowing glance, then hurried out after the others, closing the door behind her.

Gina and Dominika stood alone in the apartment.

"So," Gina finally said.

"So."

"Well, your clothes are soaking wet," Gina began, affecting her businesslike manner. "And this weather is nothing to go out in, anyway." She paused. "Why don't you stay here tonight."

Dominika hesitated. She still felt vaguely unsettled by the strapon business. Why had it upset her so?

"I can make some dinner," Gina offered. "Or breakfast, whatever."

"That is kind of you," the Polish girl said. And suddenly, she realized: *Gina is a genuinely kind person.* Dominika knew in that instant she could trust the tall brunette, even with her life. The blonde smiled.

"Hey, nice smile. That's better," Gina said.

"I like you. Very much."

Gina looked surprised. She seemed to wrestle with powerful emotions as she replied: "I like you, too."

"Good."

"Well, uh… so, are you hungry?"

Dominika smiled again and shook her head, no.

"You ready to turn in, then? I'm beat."

The blonde nodded.

* * *

Gina and her guest entered the bedroom once more.

"You can sleep in Tracy's bed, or mine," Gina said, turning around.

Dominika considered. Tracy's bed was piled with clean and dirty clothes, CDs, unopened bags of junk food…

The blonde girl turned. "How can she sleep upon this?"

"Believe it or not, she moves all that crap off every night, puts it on the floor, and in the morning lifts it back on again."

"Hmm. This seems like much work."

"Yeah."

"I will perhaps sleep with you, if you do not mind. But your bed is not so large."

"Uh, it's big enough," Gina stuttered. "Really. There's room…" The taller girl stopped as Dominika began giggling. "Okay, whatever,"

Gina continued with a wry grin. "Just get into bed."

Dominika obeyed, hopping under her host's covers. Hail and rain began beating against the bedroom window.

Gina removed her robe, and stood naked once more. She reached into the closet and withdrew folded pajamas.

"No," Dominika said.

Gina stared.

"Like that," the blonde whispered.

A moment passed that seemed like forever. The brunette finally placed the pajamas back in the closet. She flipped the light switch down. The sound of the heavy weather against the windowpane echoed in the dark room.

Dominika felt Gina crawl into bed with her. "Hi," the tall girl whispered.

In response, Dominika slid her body under her host's, kissing the first thing she found: Gina's arm. The Polish girl raised her hands and tried to pull Gina's face toward hers. Their lips found each other; their kisses, soft at first, grew more urgent as hunger possessed both of them.

Suddenly, Gina pulled away. "Wait."

Dominika gaped, speechless. Wait? Wait for what? Her eyes had adjusted to the dim room. She saw Gina, inches from her, naked. A small sheen of perspiration had covered the curvy strong body; the Italian-American girl's breasts wobbled ever so slightly with her ragged breaths.

"Okay, premier: I really like you," the host began. "The first moment I saw you, I thought I had to be careful, or else I would lose my heart to you in a second. I lose my heart really easily. I give it. I put up a good front, I'm a good actress, I come off as tough and strong and whatever, but it's all a pose. I'm incredibly sensitive, and generous."

"I know," Dominika said. She reached to hold Gina's hand.

"And that has hurt me, in the past," the brunette continued. "I knew Annabelle and I were wrong together, from the start. But I had jumped in. And I swore if I ever got out of that relationship, I would put everything up front next time. There would be no misunderstandings. So, this will be an awkward conversation, but a necessary one."

Dominika waited.

"I'm afraid if we are intimate tonight, I will fall in love with you," Gina continued finally. "I'm nearly there, already. But Dominika, I have to protect myself. I've tried casual affairs in the past, one-nighters, whatever, and it never worked. Look, I'm not asking for a declaration of love, but I know myself well enough by now that I need a commitment from you. I just got out of a long-term relationship, but I'm ready, because I think you are awesome."

The Polish girl stared, stunned. She was amazed that Gina had had the exact same relationship anxieties that had worried her also.

"And I don't do long-distance," Gina went on. "And I think you're going back to Poland after graduation. Right?"

"Yes, "Dominika whispered.

"Well, look then. This is impossible. You are returning to your country and I'll be deploying somewhere so this has no chance…"

"Wait please," Dominika interrupted. "What, 'deploying?'"

"Like, getting shipped out. I'm joining the military, okay? I haven't told anyone yet. So I guess it doesn't even matter if you were staying in America or not…"

"You are joking with me."

"I'm not joking. I called the recruiter day before yesterday. I'm meeting him tomorrow for the signup."

Silence.

"Look, there is no security in being an actress and I want to serve my country. And I'll have medical benefits, and—"

"ARE YOU CRAZY?" Dominika snapped upright in bed.

"Whoa. Way to be judgmental," Gina muttered.

"This is… this is impossible. You cannot do this thing."

"Why not?"

"Why not? Because you are an amazing actress, with incredible gifts. Did you not read your review from the newspaper? What is the matter with you?"

Gina flushed. "I don't think I like your tone."

"If I am upset, it is your fault. No one will agree with this decision. No one. You... you are so good, and you can contribute so much to your art. Your success is a foregone conclusion."

Unexpectedly, Gina laughed. "Nothing's a foregone conclusion in show business."

"Do you think you have no talent?"

"I..." the brunette looked away. She remained silent for long time. Dominika waited, staring at the naked beautiful woman in the dark.

"I have to get away," Gina said finally. "I have to do something new. Look, Dominika, you're right: no one will agree with my decision, except the recruiter. It would be nice to have at least one friend who supported me."

"The pain of your breakup with Annabelle has caused you to make this decision. Can't you see? This will be the greatest mistake of your life."

Even in the dark, Dominika could see the brunette's face bloom with anger. "Don't make me mad. I'm warning you."

"Gina, I... I lost my heart to you, too, that first day. I did not know it, but I realized it in time."

Gina looked away. She blinked, trying to control powerful emotions.

"But even if I felt nothing for you, it would still be obvious to me that you possess great gifts.

Your acting is… it is so good, I do not even have words. It has always been so, probably, yes?"

The brunette nodded, reluctantly. "Acting has always been easy for me."

"It is easy for you because you were born with a thing inside of you, a thing that some people work hard their whole lives trying to learn."

After a pause, Gina spoke. "I've always felt kind of guilty about that. Like, I know it's the only thing I can do, but why can't other people do it, too?"

"You have something unique," Dominika pressed on. "I am telling you, in the most objective way, that your success will indeed be a foregone conclusion."

Gina was quiet for a long time. Finally, she said: "You believe in me more than I believe in myself."

Dominika pulled Gina's hand to her mouth and kissed it.

"If I had somebody like you…" the brunette continued. She stopped short, looking away. Her brow furrowed.

"Gina?"

Her host did not hear her. She was thinking about something, hard.

"Okay," the brunette said finally. She spoke slowly, letting a new idea express itself. "You believe in me that much?"

"Yes!"

"Then come with me to New York."

"What?"

"After graduation. Don't go back to Poland. Listen, somebody said you were going to go to medical school back there, right? There's plenty of schools in New York. Come with me. I can't do it alone. I haven't told anyone this, either, but I got an email from a casting director who is scouting people for principal roles in a big Broadway show. She read the Boston Globe review, and tracked me down," Gina said in a rush.

Dominika's jaw dropped. "That's great!"

"Yeah!" Gina's eyes shined. Her excitement seemed almost to lift the bed off the floor. "I don't even know what the role is, but I'm sure I can do it. I've never lost an audition. Come with me!" Gina grabbed both of Dominika's hands. "I can't do it alone," she repeated. "I can't do it without you."

"But," Dominika stuttered, "my parents… my family… I promised them always that I would return. And my visa. I do not know when my student visa expires—"

"We can figure all that out," Gina interrupted. In contrast to her demeanor only minutes before, she now seemed to project total confidence. "I'll explain it to your parents. I can win them over. Wait and see."

Dominika shook her head. She could not meet Gina's gaze.

After a very long pause, Gina said, "All right."

She swiveled her body and rose out of bed.

"Where are you going?"

"I'm sleeping downstairs." She slipped her robe on, tying the belt around her waist once more. "I'm not angry, okay? Really."

"Gina." Dominika began weeping.

"Stop. Hey. This makes the best sense. We stay friends, I mean it. But I just can't… I can't have sex with someone I'm not committed to, and who is not committed to me. Not any more. This isn't an ultimatum, it's just a fact. The next time I make love, it will be with a partner."

"I want to be your partner," Dominika whispered. Tears ran down her face.

Gina touched a slow finger down the Polish girl's cheek. Then she turned to leave.

"No!" Dominika lurched forward, grabbing the taller girl around the waist and holding as tightly as she could.

"Please don't make this harder than it already is," Gina said, her voice catching.

"Don't go into the military," the blonde sobbed. "I read that American women can serve in combat positions now. If anything… if anything happened to you, it would break my life. I would die."

"They'll probably make me a secretary or something. I'll be fine. I promise."

"You don't know that!" Dominika's fingers twisted the robe's material, holding Gina even tighter. "Do not go. Do not. You will not. I won't let you!"

Gina placed gentle hands on Dominika's head. "I think… you care for me, for real, more than anybody on earth."

"I do. I do, I do." Dominika turned her wet face up to look at Gina. "I will come to New York with you. I will be your partner, your friend, your lover, everything, just please do not do this. Please."

Gina studied her. "You're overwrought. You don't know what you're saying."

"Yes I do."

"You can't promise something like this, under duress. I don't want it to be this way."

Dominika pushed her face into Gina's warm robe. "I don't care. I'm promising. I promise, for ever."

Gina pulled away quickly, let her robe drop to the floor, and re-entered the bed. "You'll come to New York with me? We'll live together, the whole thing?" Her voice rose with excitement.

"Yes." The Polish girl wiped tears from her face. "But my visa, if it expires, I cannot help that of course."

"We'll figure out the visa. Fuck the visa!" Gina grabbed Dominika in a bear hug, laughing wildly. It seemed like a great reservoir of hope and happiness had been released inside of her. "I can't believe it! I can't believe… Do you know how many nights I have wanted to be sharing a bed with you, talking to you, sharing your life? And now it's actually… it's actually going to happen." Gina stared, wide-eyed. "Is this a dream?"

The brunette said it so earnestly that Dominika laughed. "I hope not."

"I'm serious. This is way too good to be true."

"Why always when we were in the play did you ignore me?"

Gina looked down. "I was dating Annabelle, and I felt guilty, being attracted to you, and. Well. After she and I broke up, I didn't want to get hurt."

"I see."

Gina lifted herself over Dominika. "I don't want to talk any more," she whispered. "I need you. I really, really need you." She slipped her hand inside the smaller girl's pajama top and touched her breast.

Dominika felt the same shock of electricity as before. She gasped.

"What?"

"I… you touch and I feel something, like, wow."

Gina grinned. "Oh, yeah? Just wait."

Her face lowered and they kissed, a slow peck so light their lips barely touched.

"Was that a wow?" Gina murmured, pulling back.

Dominika finally opened her eyes. "I think yes." Her pupils were glassy.

Gina laughed softly and kissed her again. Their lips moved slowly, tenderly, the lightest of kisses.

Gina began massaging Dominika's breast. The Polish girl moaned.

"You," the brunette whispered, "are going to make me never get any sleep." She began unbuttoning the blonde's pajama top. "I don't know if I can go to auditions when I'm dropping from fatigue."

Dominika said nothing. She felt dizzy. Gina undid the last button and pulled her into a sitting-up position. The brunette moved her guest's arms high and pulled the pajama top off her, as if she were a child.

"Settle back, now," Gina murmured. "Make yourself comfortable." The brunette moved her own body on top of the smaller girl's, resting lightly. Her big breasts pushed against the blonde's pale skin, a warm soft pressure.

"Oh, Gina…"

"Shhh," the tall girl whispered. "Kissing time."

As they made out, Gina shifted her body to scissor her legs between Dominika's. A wet stain appeared immediately on the crotch of the blonde girl's pajama bottoms. They moved their hips against each other as they kissed, a slow sexy dance.

"I know something," Gina whispered.

"What?" Dominika breathed.

The brunette slowly arched her back, pushing her breasts toward her bedmate's face. "I know you were staring at my boobs. That time in the dressing room. The undershirt day? Yeah. You think I missed that?"

The Polish girl stared unblinking at the big firm breasts inches from her face. Gina cupped the back of Dominika's head, pulling gently. "You wanted to do this. Didn't you?"

Gina maneuvered Dominika's mouth toward her nipple. At the last moment, the blonde girl opened her lips.

"Suck," Gina whispered.

Dominika obeyed, closing her eyes. Gina's skin tasted like oil and pepper. The blonde felt the nipple grow hard under her tongue. Gina pulled her breast away and twisted to let Dominika suck the other one, all the while grinding her vulva between Dominika's legs.

"Oh yeah," the brunette moaned. "God. And we'll get to do this every night? I'm attending mass in the morning. I'm lighting a candle."

The blonde girl sucked harder. She slid her hands over Gina's body, finally exploring with tentative fingers the area beneath the brunette's navel. Her fingers touched wetness.

"I'm so hungry for you," Gina gasped. She hopped off Dominika, threw the covers off the bed, and yanked off the girl's pajama bottoms. "I can't wait any more. Sit up. Sit up! There's no room on this stupid fucking bed."

Naked, Dominika struggled to obey. She felt her shoulders press against the headboard as she sat awkwardly on a pillow. Before she could adjust herself, Gina's mouth was between her legs.

Dominika inhaled, her eyes rolling. It was more erotic than anything she had ever imagined. Gina ate her with abandon, moaning and sliding her face up and down. The blonde realized suddenly that even if she asked Gina to stop, Gina wouldn't. The tall girl had let go. She had no more restraint left in her. Dominika felt a buzz begin inside her body, a tremor whose vibrations grew more powerful with every passing second until she was shaking like a leaf. "Ginaaaa…"

The orgasm hit her. Her eyes popped open. She heard a scream, so loud it scared her. As it died down, Dominika realized that the noise had come from her.

Looking down finally, she saw Gina touching her vulva, staring at it. The brunette's fingertips ran through the fine blonde hair like it was a holy thing. "Oh girl," her host whispered. "You are so beautiful."

As Dominika tried to catch her breath, she watched Gina's pretty face move forward again. Her tongue tasted the small vagina once more.

"Gina, I can't… Not again… It's too soon…"

The brunette ignored her, licking and sucking insatiably. Dominika emitted a sobbing sound, glancing away. She saw herself reflected in the bedroom mirror. Her body was in an impossibly contorted position, legs splayed wide, with Gina between them, in control. Dominika stared at the image, knowing that no matter how many nights she and Gina shared in the future, this night was special and she would remember this image for the rest of her life. The rest of their lives. Dominika closed her eyes. She touched her lover's head.

"Tell me to eat it," Gina whispered.

"Eat it," Dominika said faintly.

Gina did. Dominika felt cold sweat break out over her body. At length, her second orgasm gave her no warning, ripping and wrenching her like a plaything: "Aaaahhhhh," the blonde cried, trying to escape. "Gina. Stop. STOP!"

"Sorry," the brunette murmured, breaking off. She sat up on her knees and pulled Dominika's limp body back down onto the mattress as if the blonde were a rag doll. "I'm afraid we're going to be doing a lot of this." Gina licked and sucked Dominika's rising and falling breasts, hard. "Any objections?" Smiling, the brunette kissed her guest on the lips, a loud smack. "I can't hear you."

Dominika's eyes remained closed as she hyperventilated, in and out.

"Yes, I'll take that as no objections." Dominika felt her host crawling around on the mattress. "Poor girl. So much sex. Who knew Gina was so demanding?"

The blonde felt Gina's warm face between her legs: soft gentle nuzzles. The brunette was indeed giving her a break, of sorts, only nuzzling. It felt soothing. When finally Dominika had caught her breath, she opened her eyes.

Gina had straddled her in a 69. A perfect triangle of trimmed dark curls hovered just inches above Dominika's face. The brunette kept nuzzling her in an easy, lazy way.

Dominika stared at Gina's thatch. *And now I kiss hers? Like she kissed mine?* The blonde swallowed. This was something… she had not expected. How did one do it? Performance anxiety seized her. She desperately wanted to give Gina an orgasm. But this was all new.

Hesitantly, Dominika lifted her face and gave Gina's bush the lightest of kisses. Gina sighed.

The blonde rubbed her fingers through the pubic hair. Finally, she kissed again.

After a while, Dominika began licking Gina in a slow, unhurried rhythm. Her hands slid up and over to hold Gina's butt. Dominika began to relax. She was enjoying herself. Gina tasted fresh and clean. It felt good to lick her. She wished she could see the two of them in the mirror again.

After what could have been hours, or only minutes, the blonde girl felt the body above her own stiffen. Gina's breaths became labored. *Is this it?* Dominika thought. Excitement quickened her pulse. *Can I do it? Can I bring her to orgasm?*

It seemed so. Gina started to moan. Her shoulders and head began collapsing upon the blonde girl's thighs.

Dominika's passion rose. She tried to kiss deeper, using her tongue. Gina's clitoris, hard and angry, seemed to demand her attention. She kissed and licked the tiny organ, then sucked, pulling Gina's hips down lower.

The brunette moaned louder. "Oh God… sweetheart. Don't stop…" Gina's body trembled. After a moment, she voiced a long loud cry.

Presently, Gina lifted herself. She turned around and flopped next to her lover.

"Was that… good?" the blonde asked.

Gina's eyes opened. "Good? Honey. What books have you been reading?"

Dominika shoved her. "None! What kind of girl do you think I am?"

"The best kind." The brunette sighed, draping her arms and legs over her guest.

Dominika focused upon her host's breasts, staring and squeezing gently.

"You're a boob girl," Gina said.

"I am?"

"Oh yeah."

"Hmm. Is this a good thing?"

"Very good."

They kissed for a while.

"I'd love to do it all night," Gina finally added, yawning. "And maybe I will, next time. But after today… I'm just beat. No offense, but I need some sleep. And you too, I bet."

"Yes. However…"

Gina looked at her, puzzled.

"I think… yes."

"Yes, what?"

"Before we sleep. This… strapon." Dominika twisted her head up to look at where it lay on the desk, still covered by Gina's towel.

"What about it? I'll throw it away tomorrow."

"No, you misunderstand. I know this is not rational, but I want to… consecrate this, us, tonight. Our first night."

Gina stared, uncomprehending.

"You never used this with your ex-girlfriend?" the blonde asked.

"No, like I said. It's never been used at all."

"I know Annabelle was in this bed. With you." Dominika glanced at the mattress.

"Aw. Look, I'm sorry…"

"No! That's not what I mean. I want to do something with you, share something she never had with you."

Gina's eyebrows lifted. "Are you saying you want me to buckle up the strapon?"

Dominika hesitated. "If I do not do this tonight, I may never again have the courage. And you said you were interested in it, it was something you wanted to do. Yes? Wait, let me finish. I know we are not married. But…" She paused, and glanced again. "It would feel maybe like a wedding night. And I am scared of the strapon, it frightens me, I don't know why. But for that reason, I want to face it."

"I'm not sure I'm following this. But just so we're clear: you want me to put it on?"

Dominika, pale, nodded.

"Okay. You're sure?"

"Yes."

Gina rose from the bed. Setting the covering towel aside, she lifted the phallus and its belt from the desk, displaying it to Dominika. "Here it iiii—iiissss," she said, grinning.

The blonde girl, looking stressed, did not smile.

Gina stepped into velcro straps and pulled them tight around her waist. Even in the dark, the dildo wobbling from her crotch looked shiny and new.

Dominika slowly sat up. She waddled on her knees to the side of the bed, staring.

Gina paused, unsure what to do next.

Finally, Dominika reached her hand toward the phallus. Gina approached. The blonde ran her fingers lightly up and down the dildo, unblinking.

Then she held it gently by its base. Closing her eyes, she opened her mouth. Her pink tongue darted out and touched the tip.

Gina sucked air into her lungs. She watched Dominika run her tongue ever so lightly over the head of the dildo, exploring, before finally moving her lips over it.

"Wow," Gina breathed. "Girl. You are full of surprises."

Dominika gave no sign she had heard. She sucked the head slowly, gently, growing used to the artificial phallus's feel and taste.

"That is the hottest thing I have ever seen,"

Gina whispered. "I just want to…"

In response, Dominika stopped. She laid back on the sheet, lifting and spreading her knees.

"Sure?"

Dominika nodded.

The brunette crawled onto the bed, the dildo wobbling dangerously. She squatted between Dominika's legs. Massaging the slippery blonde bush up and down with the tip, she finally began to slide the phallus inside.

Dominika's mouth fell open.

"Okay?"

The Polish girl nodded.

Gina slid it in deeper.

"Oh," Dominika gasped. She opened her arms to Gina. The brunette lowered her shoulders and kissed her lover. Dominika wrapped her arms around Gina's torso. The bigger girl began to rock her hips back and forth, gently at first, then with stronger thrusts.

The young women stared into each other's eyes as their bodies moved.

"I love you," Gina whispered.

"I love you," Dominika said. "So much." She gasped again with one of Gina's thrusts.

Gina kissed Dominika's shoulder, moving her hips in a rhythm of strong strokes. The bed made a protesting noise, *creak-creak-creak*. Dominika stared up at the ceiling. She felt an orgasm's approach, different than before, deeper. When it finally arrived, she let out a high moan. Her body spasmed and convulsed.

Gina stopped. "Are you okay?" she asked, worried.

She is so tender, Dominika thought. The blonde held Gina's face with both hands, kissing her lips again and again. "Yes."

After Gina had put away the strapon and arranged the bedcovers over the two of them, she glanced at the window. "It's morning already."

Dominika smiled. "Then tomorrow is today."

"Can I spoon you? Can you sleep like that?"

"I don't know. But we can try."

Dominika turned onto her side, facing away. Gina wrapped her arms around the smaller girl. In moments, they were asleep. Gina held her lover, the Polish girl who had come to America to discover life and push her boundaries, and who had succeeded beyond even her own expectations.

The End

Thanks for reading! If you have time, please review *Chilled*. I read every review, and I appreciate honest feedback!

If you enjoyed this book, you may also enjoy

The Beard

By Anne Eton

When tall, pretty Kelly interviews at Washington D.C.'s premier LGBT-centric lobbying firm, she claims she has a girlfriend. Nothing could be further from the truth; she's never even kissed a girl. Kelly's hired. However, a suspicious co-worker keeps inquiring about her girlfriend. To keep her lies straight, Kelly bases her fictional partner on Anna, an aggressive, gorgeous lesbian friend of a friend. But when the firm's annual Christmas party looms, Kelly's forced to produce her mysterious girlfriend. The real Anna agrees to be Kelly's "beard"—her fake date. But at the party, alcohol flows… and Anna's all over Kelly. Kelly pretends to her office mates that her "girlfriend's" advances are perfectly normal—even as she feels her resistance to the beautiful woman melting away.

The Beard is a comedy with sexy scenes and some explicit passages.

Excerpt follows!

The Beard

Excerpt:

Kelly stumbled, tipsy. Anna guided her with a sure hand to the office supply room, opening the door and escorting her inside.

"Hey! Office supplies," Kelly said with false cheer. She looked around nervously. "You need some gel pens? Ha, ha!"

Anna smirked. She shut the door behind them and pressed the doorknob's button, locking it.

"Or paper clips, or toner," Kelly babbled, casually backing away. "It's a regular Staples in here!"

"Yes," Anna replied. The blonde gave Anna a sexy look and flipped a wall switch. The room went dark.

"I think we should talk about expectations," Kelly said in the pitch black, as if discussing the price of a car. "I admit, I did sort of use you for my own ends…"

"Yes."

Kelly felt Anna's hands. The tall girl backed away; she came up against waist-high pallets of paper boxes.

"You see," Kelly gasped, "I know we're supposed to be pretending that you're my girlfriend—"

"Yes... yes..." Anna murmured. She began slipping Kelly's dress up as the taller girl moved awkwardly against the immovable cartons.

Also by Anne Eton

ABOUT THE AUTHOR

I write first-time F/F erotic romance. I love what I do!

If you would like to know when I publish new books, please join my New Release Mailing List, at my site! I don't share my readers' email with anyone, for any reason.

www.anneeton.com

Thanks for reading!

Anne